Claudius Bald Eagle

Come with me now to Thunder Wood, one of the grand old forests of our Mother Earth. There are mysteries in such a place as Thunder Wood. Come and meet Claudius Bald Eagle, Edward Moose, Jimmy Racoon and Balfour Scabious the Repulsively Ugly Troll!

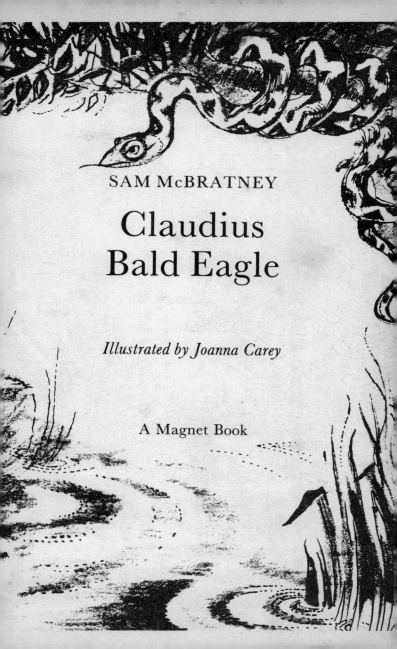

SAM McBRATNEY

Claudius
Bald Eagle

Illustrated by Joanna Carey

A Magnet Book

Also by Sam McBratney

Colvin and the Snake Basket
Jimmy Zest
Zesty
Uncle Charlie Weasel and the Cuckoo Bird

First published in 1987
by Methuen Children's Books Ltd
This Magnet edition published 1988
by Methuen Children's Books
A division of OPG Services Limited
Michelin House, 81 Fulham Road, London SW3 6RB
Text copyright © 1987 Sam McBratney
Illustrations copyright © 1987 Joanna Carey

Printed in Great Britain by
Cox & Wyman Ltd, Reading

ISBN 0 416 10322 7

1

Come with me now to Thunder Wood, one of the grand old forests of our Mother Earth.

Thunder Wood is a place of great natural beauty. Beneath a vast canopy of ageing redwoods and sprightly young conifers she hides from the common view her peaceful lakes, her boiling rivers, and her gloomy places. From the ground, looking up, you can see the trees soar like the arches of mighty cathedrals, enclosing within themselves the kind of silence that makes you feel small.

There are mysteries in such a place as Thunder Wood. There are also quite a number of birds, mammals and reptiles. These living creatures include not only Claudius Bald Eagle and Edward Moose, but also the likes of Jimmy Racoon, Long Tom John the Alligator, Quincy Porcupine, Curly-Wurly the Intelligent Snake — and many more.

Balfour Scabious also lives in Thunder Wood. His house is a tumbledown shack deep in the unexplored part of the forest. Balfour is very rarely seen, which is a good thing. He is not a great natural beauty.

No one knows how long the Repulsively Ugly Troll has been living in Thunder Wood, or how he came to possess his magic powers. This is a rear view of him, featuring not only his conch-like ears and the knob on his tail (which he keeps well-polished with a wire brush), but also the jelly-soft eye in the back of his head. Should you make a mistake and gaze into his hideous horned face with the black-and-orange eyes, you will never be quite the same again — or so *he* says.

Although Balfour Scabious is extremely ugly, and rather proud of it, his heart is kind, his manners are gentle and he always makes a point of sitting with his back to his visitors.

Right now the beavers are on their lunch-break in Thunder Wood. They built the dam on the lake. One of the floating logs, by the way, isn't a log at all, it's Long Tom John trying to sneak up on his next meal. He does not have a kind heart and will eat anything except porcupines. On one famous occasion he even sneaked up on his own tail, and bit it.

All who saw this happen laughed so much that they lost weight. And there's Curly-Wurly the Intelligent Snake. She enjoys good conversation and rational argument. Oh, and there are Claudius Bald Eagle and Edward Moose.

Claudius Bald Eagle and Edward Moose have been friends for a very long time. They met completely by accident. Claudius, in his youth, was a wild Bald Eagle who used to terrorise the local rooks just for fun. He plucked out their tail-feathers, dive-bombed their nests, hijacked tit-bits in mid-air and generally made a total nuisance of himself. He felt entitled to do these anti-social things because he was a Bald Eagle, Emperor of the Skies, while the rooks were just plain ordinary old rooks.

As a matter of fact, Claudius felt superior to everything that moved — not just rooks. In his opinion the sun rose and the wind blew only for him. You can easily imagine his consternation when one day those ordinary old rooks rose out of the tree-tops as one, and ambushed him. It was a rare and wonderful sight to behold Claudius Bald Eagle pursued across the sky by two hundred angry inferiors, until, exhausted and humiliated, he took refuge at last in the low branches of an old, dead tree.

The shame of it! Tears of self-pity scalded his eyes, and he cried out at the injustice of it all.

'I, Claudius Bald Eagle, driven out by a bunch of *rooks*! BWAAAK. How will I ever show my face ... whoops.'

The tree on which he was standing suddenly and unaccountably tilted to one side. He almost fell off it. Claudius clutched tightly with his talons as the tree lurched violently once again, this time raising him high into the air.

At first Claudius simply closed his eyes in panic. Crazy rooks and walking trees! What is happening to the world this day! he wondered. The Bald Eagle had travelled at least ten metres before it dawned on him that he was perched on the antlers of a moose.

A full-grown moose!

'Hey, take it easy,' he said. 'I thought you were a blasted tree.'

'Sorree,' said the moose. He had a deep and mournful — almost musical — voice.

The moose slowed to a gentle walk. It was a strange sensation for Claudius, to be transported along a forest path with that peculiar rocking-rolling-plodding gait. He quite liked it; this was restful locomotion.

'Listen, pal,' he said craftily, 'I don't want to be a burden or anything, but . . . could I sit up here for a while?'

'Why?'

'Well the fact is, you're looking at a tired Bald Eagle. I've just been chased by a bunch of crazy rooks and the name's Claudius, by the way.'

'Mine's Edward,' responded Moose.

'Nice meeting you,' said Claudius, and fell asleep.

In this way, the partnership began. Perhaps 'partnership' is not quite the word for it, since — as the other forest animals quickly pointed out — Edward did all the work while that Bald Eagle just sat there. In the weeks that followed, Claudius went where Edward went, sometimes quickly, sometimes slowly, but always at Moose-pace. When he wanted to rest, Claudius perched low down; when he wanted excitement, he perched high up. He left the antlers only to pounce on the occasional mouse, and to while away the hours, he told Edward the sensational story of his life.

Manifestly, it was a marvellous thing to have your own personal, walking tree.

2

'Personally,' said Jimmy Racoon down by the lake, 'I think it's a scandal. He takes that Bald Eagle creature with him wherever he goes. If you ask me, Moose is just being used.'

He was enjoying a gossip with Beaver and Curly-Wurly. They had already discussed the new Yellow Monsters which had come to live on the other side of the lake. Apparently there were two of the Monsters and the beasts were tearing up trees with their gleaming metal jaws. In Curly-Wurly's opinion the Monsters probably had something to do with the Repulsively Ugly Troll. But now the conversation had turned to the subject of Claudius Bald Eagle.

None of the three had a good word to say about him.

'I agree,' said Curly-Wurly, who resembled

a question mark as she dangled upside-down from a tree. 'The other day I saw him sheltering underneath Moose during a shower of rain. That arrogant creature was using Edward to keep himself *dry*.'

'Let me tell you what I have seen,' said Jimmy Racoon, in the tone of one who is about to speak the unspeakable. 'I have seen Edward scraping through the leaves with his antlers in order to dig up mice for that creature. Can you imagine?'

Each one had a mental image of their good friend Edward, with his great heavy head, his sad brown eyes and his turned-down mouth, shamelessly employed as a rake. And they did not like it.

'Lazy idle brute,' murmured Beaver. She was on her lunchbreak and believed strongly that everybody should work hard for a living.

'Mind you,' Curly-Wurly cocked her head intelligently, 'perhaps Moose is like many other reserved and lonely creatures. He may be pleased to have a chatty friend with whom to share jokes and exchange opinions about life in general.'

Jimmy Racoon blinked. In his opinion there was nothing worse than a smart-alec snake.

'Here they come now,' said Beaver. 'Just look at the pair of them — Master and Slave.'

As Moose emerged from the forest margins, Claudius Bald Eagle swayed imperiously on the tip of the highest antler.

'Good morning, Edward,' said Beaver.

'Thank you,' responded Moose.

'What's the water like today, chaps?' called Claudius in a friendly way. 'Rather on the cool side, I fancy?'

'Why — are you going swimming?' asked Jimmy Racoon, not without a hint of sarcasm.

'In a manner of speaking. Moose and I are bound for the other side of the lake to have a look at these so-called Yellow Monsters. Let's go, pal, tally-ho!'

Encouraged by a rap on his forehead, delivered by Claudius's beak, Edward lumbered into the water until it lapped his stomach, at which point Jimmy Racoon swished his tail in outrage.

'Wait a minute. Do you mean to tell me that you intend to cross the water on Edward's antlers?'

'What's wrong with that?' Claudius was genuinely amazed.

'You can *fly*, that's what's wrong with it.

You've got wings, right? So use them! Flap, flap!'

The indignant Jimmy Racoon stood on his back legs and performed an imitation of a bird.

'And what is more,' said Curly-Wurly, 'you behave as if you own Moose. And you don't. You are a newcomer to these parts and your arrogance is insufferable.'

Claudius blinked. He did not understand such language. 'What do you mean?'

'I mean,' continued Curly-Wurly, 'that you look down your nose at the rest of us. You should be more humble — like Moose.'

'Tell the lazy idle vulture where to get off, Edward,' advised Beaver.

Poor Edward seemed rather bewildered by the sudden fuss. Claudius, however, fluffed out his feathers in an effort to look enormous.

'Listen, Snake, I'm used to looking down on my fellow creatures. I don't feel humble. I'm not humble, I'm a Bald Eagle! And mind your own business. Edward needs me, I'm his lookout.'

'Lookout!' exploded Jimmy Racoon. 'Huh!'

'Yes, lookout. He may be struck on the side by a chewed-up log — one of *yours*, Beaver.

You didn't think of that, did you? Ed's my buddy, he needs me. Let's go, pal. *Mush.*'

Whereupon Edward waded into the water and began to swim, followed by cries of 'Shame, shame,' from the bank.

That journey across the sunken clouds of the tranquil lake ought to have been a rewarding experience for Claudius: instead, it was quite ruined for him by that nastiness on the bank. Halfway across he was seized by a fit of temper.

'Did you hear them? The cheek, the cheek! I tell you this, Ed, I'd hate to be a beaver.'

Claudius shuddered.

'Why?' panted Edward. His chin rested on the water as he pedalled furiously with his feet.

'Just look at them. Always on the go! You want to know what's wrong with beavers, I'll tell you — they don't know how to *relax*. How'd you like to spend your life chewing up trees, could you be happy that way?'

'I don't know,' said Edward. 'I've been thinking about happiness quite a lot recently. I don't think I'm happy. I sometimes think that maybe I've never been happy, not really.'

'Yea, well don't think too much, it only

causes problems. And take it easy, pal, you're splashing me.'

After a few more forthright opinions from Claudius on the subject of busybody racoons, they reached the shallows at the other side of the lake. Moose rose dripping from the water (his passenger was dry as a bone) and stared apprehensively into the gloomy forest ahead. This, after all, was new territory for him.

'Do you think there really are such things as Yellow Monsters?' he asked softly.

'Could be,' said Claudius. 'Don't whisper, Moose, it makes everybody nervous. Straight ahead at walking pace, and take your orders from me.'

All of a sudden, something small and spiky sprinted from the bushes. Neither Claudius nor Moose recognised Quincy Porcupine for a moment or two, because they had never seen her running before.

Quincy looked terrified.

'Where are you going in such a hurry, Quincy?' inquired Edward.

'Some other time, Moose. Cheerio!'

In seconds, Quincy disappeared into the distance followed by two fat little porcupine babies.

What could have frightened her? wondered Moose. Quincy did not scare easily, she simply turned her back and sprayed a few quills in the general direction of the enemy, who usually got the painful message that Quincy should be left alone.

'She must have seen the Yellow Monsters,' whispered Edward.

Advancing now with great care, they took the widest possible path through the woods on account of Edward's antlers, which had a tendency to catch awkwardly on snags. More

18

than once Claudius was obliged to duck under a swinging branch.

'Watch where you're going, pal, you nearly knocked me off my ...'

'Perch' he was about to say. But the word stuck in his throat when his eyes lit on the incredible creatures up ahead.

Two of them. Brutes!

'They *are* yellow,' said Moose.

'And boy, are they monsters!' croaked Claudius.

Working as a pair, the ruthless Yellow Monsters seemed to be demolishing Thunder Wood with no bother at all. One ran at trees and simply bowled them over as easily as stalks of grass; the other scooped mouthfuls of earth into its massive jaws, dumped them, and came back for more. And all the while the hungry brutes snorted, clanked and belched smoke like nothing ever seen or even dreamed about before.

'What are they doing here?' hissed Claudius. 'Eh? What are they, answer me that!'

'I don't know.' Edward was staring. He seemed fascinated by these yellow things. 'Do you think we should say Hello to them?'

'My innocent friend,' cried Claudius, 'I'm

not even saying Goodbye. Get us out of here –
quick!'

One week later, the bulldozers had gone.
A fortnight after that, an idyllic log cabin
had appeared on the site which they had effic-
iently prepared. This was Harry and Enid's
weekend home on a fringe of Thunder Wood.

To begin with, Enid had not shared
Harry's enthusiasm for a place in the country.
It wasn't even the country, for heaven sakes,
it was a raw, primeval forest full of beasts.

'Harry,' she had said, 'you are not taking
me to the back of beyond.'

'Enid, Thunder Wood is not the back of
beyond.'

'If it's not the back it's the front of beyond,
Harry – and what about the bears?'

What about the blasted bears, thought
Harry, and went right ahead with his plans.
In the end, so that Enid should feel in touch
with civilisation, what he built was not so
much a log cabin as a country mansion.
Harry's place had running water, electricity
and central heating, as well as many, many
little structural extras like a billiard room,
saunas, a double garage and a landing pad on
the roof for his private chopper. (Harry had

made a lot of money in the oil business and could afford to think big.) There was also a large silver dish in the garden which received signals from passing satellites. Enid loved to watch television.

She was not at all like her husband Harry. Enid ran a branch of a national bank, and when Friday came all she wanted was a quiet place to put her feet up, sip an occasional sherry and undergo a gentle mind-wash by watching some television Soap. Not for the first time, she thought that her husband was getting carried away with his latest hair-brained scheme.

But she accepted the situation. The house in Thunder Wood was impossibly large, but Harry supplied her with maids to do the chores, and so far she had not seen any bears.

One day she heard the helicopter landing in the front garden, followed by the sound of Harry's voice giving instructions.

'Go easy, there. Careful with those boxes, you guys, those things cost money. They came all the way from Turkey, you know.'

Turkey? Enid raised her eyebrows and went out to see whatever next. She saw Harry in his hunting jacket standing among boxes and boxes of gorgeous blue tiles.

'Harry – what are you doing now?'

Harry beamed. 'Enid, look what I got. Tiles. All the way from Turkey.'

'What are they for?'

'Outdoor swimming pool, didn't I mention it? I got the plans here. Which do you like best, the ordinary rectangle or kidney-shape?'

Glory be! thought Enid. She said, 'Harry, I think you have to ask yourself whether we really need a swimming pool out here. I mean, why not make do with a rain barrel?'

'Enid, don't be a small thinker. Swim Every Day, Keep Your Worries Away – you know that's true.' He delivered a small peck on her cheek. 'Fix dinner for half eight tonight, dear, I'm going hunting.'

Harry was not at all like his wife Enid. He did not come out to Thunder Wood to do as little as possible for a quiet weekend – he came because he fancied himself as a backwoods-man. Each weekend he slipped into a Davy Crockett hat and a military-styled hunting jacket – one of those with toggles, zips and pockets everywhere. In one of those pockets he kept the little brass key to his gun cabinet.

Harry had thirty-two guns. The great

hobby of his life was stalking creatures of the wild wood, and shooting them dead.

3

It was inevitable that sooner or later a question would come to be asked: how and why did Moose get to feeling so miserable?

Everybody noticed it. The spring went out of his step, a dullness came into his eye and he mooched about the forest as if the problems of the world lay upon his bony shoulders. Jimmy Racoon wished him Good Morning one fine day and received the shocking reply, 'Is it? That's what *you* think.'

It was all very puzzling. Edward had never been the most cheerful creature to live in Thunder Wood; he did not chitter aimlessly like the squirrels, or giggle like the beavers on their lunchbreak, or guffaw with Long Tom John – but at least he could always raise a smile for a friend. Until now. He was quiet and moody, and appeared to think deeply about . . . well, nobody knew what he thought about. Beaver alleged that Moose had far too much time to brood on the Meaning of Life.

'Hard work, that's the answer,' declared Beaver. 'He should keep himself busy. You don't see many beavers with long faces.'

'I'd say that Moose was suffering from an allergy,' said Curly-Wurly.

'Allergy! Stuff and nonsense. What tripe!' said Jimmy Racoon.

Naturally enough, Claudius Bald Eagle did not fail to notice the change which had come over his large friend. Moose just lay about and wouldn't take him anywhere.

'What is the matter with you anyway?' he asked impatiently (Moose had just failed to laugh at one of his jokes). 'You're not much fun any more, Moose, you lie about like a bag of bones. Are you sick or something?'

'No.'

Edward stared into space with round un-blinking eyes. A little cloud of midges settled on his eyelids. One flick of his tail would have sent them packing, but Moose didn't care.

'What exactly are you thinking about?' inquired Claudius.

'If you must know, I'm thinking of the Yellow Monsters. I'm just wondering whether they enjoy being yellow.'

25

Man, this is serious, thought Claudius. 'What does it matter! Who cares whether they like being yellow or whether they hate it? Come for a roll in the mud, you know how much you like a roll in the mud.'

'No,' said Edward. 'I'm depressed.'

'Depressed? What's that?'

'I'm unhappy.'

'How can you be unhappy when you've got me for a friend?'

'All the same,' said Edward, 'I am very unhappy and I don't like myself any more.'

Claudius Bald Eagle was genuinely astonished by such talk. Since he loved himself absolutely, and believed that he was perfect, he could not easily understand what it was like to be self-critical.

'I think I would quite like to be a Yellow Monster,' said Edward.

'Well you can't be a Yellow Monster,' said Claudius bluntly, 'you're a moose, so snap out of it! And quit humping round the place like a great lump of misery.'

But Edward did not 'snap out of it'. If anything, that moose became more morose than ever.

One sunny day he came down to the lake to drink. Long Tom John happened to be stretched out in his path. That alligator lay with his jaws gaping open and his eyes shut tight as he basked in the sun, and little birds ran up and down his back feeding on insects and ticks. Suddenly, the bliss of the moment was shattered. Edward ran at him, picked up Long Tom John in his antlers, and pitched him broadside into the lake.

The beavers were pop-eyed, never having seen the like of it: an alligator assaulted by an easy-going moose! As Long Tom John surfaced, his tail churned with such fury that the water seemed to boil.

'What was that for? What did I do? I'll get you for this, Moose. Answer me. Eh?'

'I felt like it,' said Moose, stooping to drink.

When the fuss had died down, when Long Tom John had finished gnashing his mouthful of teeth, Curly-Wurly crept from under the bush where she had thoughtfully observed these strange events, and engaged Moose in conversation.

Unlike Claudius Bald Eagle, who talked only about Claudius Bald Eagle, Curly-Wurly encouraged Edward to talk about himself. She asked him subtle questions, and she listened to his answers.

'I think,' said Moose gravely, 'that part of my problem is ... well, I'm large and rather boring, really. Dull. I'm basically quite dull.'

Hmm, thought Curly-Wurly. Low self-image.

'A little while ago,' continued Moose, 'my friend Claudius Bald Eagle and myself saw two monsters across the lake. They were yellow and they looked happy. I don't understand the art of being happy. Sometimes I think to myself, "Moose, you will be a moose for ever." But I don't expect you to understand.'

'Oh but I do,' said Curly-Wurly, folding herself into coils. 'No self-confidence. It's really quite common.'

'Is it?'

'Indeed. What exactly is wrong with you? I mean . . . which bit of you annoys you most, is it your tail, or your feet, or . . . ?'

Moose wasn't sure.

'I'd like to be red,' he said eventually.

'*Red*? All over?'

'I think if I were red, I would be happy.'

Curly-Wurly shuddered. A red moose! The thought was really quite startling, for she suddenly imagined a world full of pink squirrels, purple porcupines and gaudy skunks.

'And,' added Moose, 'I don't like my antlers very much either.'

'They're very fine antlers.'

'Well, yes. But they get tangled up in

things. You're a snake, you have no idea what a bother they can be.'

If I were you, thought Curly-Wurly, I would send that baldy-headed eagle back into the branches of a real tree, where he belongs. Out loud, she said, 'If that's all that's bothering you, why don't you visit the Repulsively Ugly Troll? He'll make them smaller for you. He'll get rid of them altogether if you're *that* miserable.'

'You think he could?'

'He knows magic, doesn't he? See you around, Moose, here comes your feathered friend.'

As Curly-Wurly screwed herself through gaps in a pile of stones, Claudius dropped breathlessly from the sky. He landed like an expert on a tip of Edward's antlers and launched into an account of how he had conquered and devoured two skinny rodents.

'You should have been there, Ed my boy, I was terrific. POW and ZAP – I got one with each foot. How've you been?'

'So-so,' said Edward. 'I've just been talking to Curly-Wurly and she has some very interesting ideas.'

'Oh yeah? What kind of ideas?'

'She thinks I should change my image.'

Never trust a snake, thought Claudius. 'Forget your image, pal, all you need is fattening up a bit. Come on, I've seen a great place for rolling in the mud. You'll love it, buddy boy.'

'Well all right. I *do* like a roll in the mud.'

Off they raced together in a thrilling chase through the forest highways. Claudius Bald Eagle settled himself on the extreme tip of the very highest antler and allowed the cool wind to stream through his open feathers.

'Yippeeee!' he cried, exhilarated, 'this is the good old high-steppin' Moose we used to know. Mush, my buddy-boy – *mush*!'

4

Neither Claudius nor Edward knew that someone was watching them.

Deep among the bushes, the silent observer held his breath and pacified his beating heart, for he had never set eyes on such a glorious creature. Sheer perfection of any kind often has an emotional impact on people, and so it was with Harry. He wanted to shoot it.

Harry was returning to Enid empty-handed after a fishing trip when he saw the moose. Actually, he really only saw the antlers, the rest of the animal's mud-spattered body didn't interest him.

What a pair of antlers! Harry felt his eyes strain like buttons on a tight shirt as they contemplated that forked symmetry, that soaring grace, that blatant virility ... 'Harry,' said a still, small voice inside his head, 'be aware that you are looking at one of Nature's masterpieces.'

For a brief moment, Harry's mind escaped from the forest and darted across the miles to his home in the Big City. He saw himself with his back to a roaring fire in the dog grate, entertaining guests while he smoked a cigar and sipped port wine beneath those antlers spread across his wall.

'I want that moose,' said Harry. He said it quietly and with reverence, but he said it with passion. All the way back to the log cabin his fingers toyed with the little brass key of his gun cabinet.

Harry and Enid dined late that evening after playing a game of Monopoly by the light of a crystal chandelier. The velvet curtains were tightly-drawn across the double-glazed windows and a log fire glowed within the Italian marble fireplace; and yet, sitting at table, they heard the wind soughing among the trees outside. Owls hooted. Coyotes bayed the moon. Mothwings flailed the window panes. The nocturnal wilderness was talking.

Harry shook out the folds of his napkin and leaned to one side so that the maid could fill his plate with salmon (from the freezer).

'Enid,' he said, 'I kid you not, the moose I

saw had antlers *that* big. Believe me.' And he stretched out his hands as far as they would go.

'You've caught fish that big, Harry. So you say.'

'Enid, you have never seen anything like it. Imagine how something like that would look above the mantelpiece back home. It would just knock 'em out.'

'Harry,' Enid pointed out, 'you already have a Picasso above the mantelpiece back home.'

'I can stick the Picasso in the hall.'

'Why not just leave the Picasso and let the moose alone – they're his antlers.'

Harry glared down the table. Clearly, he was far from pleased that his wife was thinking small again.

'What kind of a statement is that? "They're his antlers".'

'All I mean is, if you want something new for the mantelpiece, get a cuckoo clock.'

'Are you stupid? You can't shoot cuckoos, they're too small. I want that moose.'

'If the antlers are as big as you say they are ... '

'They're bigger. *Bigger*! They're as long as this table, I'm telling you.'

'... then they won't go through our doors.'

'I'll take down the doors. I'll build new doors.'

'Harry, the room is too small.'

'So what!' cried Harry, as he screwed up his napkin in an agitated fist. 'In that case I'll build a new *house*.'

The maid, who had grown nervous, curtseyed and slid out of the room. Enid continued with her salmon in silence while Harry gave her a lecture on how to track a moose.

After dinner he cleaned all his guns.

5

'Ed my buddy,' pleaded Claudius Bald Eagle, 'don't do this to me. Please. Look at me, pal, I'm down on my knees and I'm begging you.'

'I have to,' said Edward. 'I'm not happy with myself and I need a change. I have explained all this to you many times, Claudius. This is the only way.'

'But not your *antlers*. Change something else. Oh man, this is serious.'

Claudius wandered around in circles, a bewildered and pathetic figure. Desperately he looked up into his large friend's eyes.

'Give me a break, pal, where will I sit?'

'I don't know. Perhaps you could sit up a tree.'

'But trees don't *move*.'

'I'm sorry, Claudius. Perhaps you could use your wings,' suggested Edward.

'You mean ... fly?'

'Yes.'

Claudius was no longer keen on flying; it left him short of breath and he'd put on a lot of weight while riding around on Edward's antlers. He said, 'You've been listening to that blasted snake. I hope you realise that this is very selfish of you, Moose.'

'I suppose it is,' said Edward gravely, 'but I can't help it.'

That snake! Claudius fumed inwardly. That blasted snake-in-the-grass, that elongated mud-stirring boneless good-for-nothing....

'Listen, Edward, I got an idea. This is good, this is really good. Change your tail! Ask the Repulsively Ugly Troll to give you something nice and fancy with feathers. *Tail* feathers, Moose, think of it!'

Edward Moose paused to think about changing his tail to red and yellow feathers, but not for long. He decided his tail was okay. He ambled off to roll in some mud while Claudius went looking for that snake Curly-Wurly.

In all honesty, Claudius was upset as he hopped from tree to tree, wheezing all the way. In all his life, this was the first time anyone had ever said No to the Bald Eagle. He didn't like it. He wasn't used to it. And it hurt. He saw only too clearly that his whole style of life was about to change.

Moose was getting rid of his antlers. No more would he, Claudius Bald Eagle, lurch madly through the sun-speckled glades of Thunder Wood. No more would Moose rake his antlers through the leaves and turn up juicy tit-bits, or ferry him gladly over river and lake. No, the old pilot had received his marching orders and oh man, this was cruel!

Sitting on those antlers had given him such a sense of well-being and power. Alone among birds he had enjoyed his personal, individualised form of transport – he had been unique. Claudius had no doubt what-ever that he was talked about for miles around, and the envy of all.

And now . . . ? Claudius Bald Eagle sniffed, and then stiffened with rage. There, sunning herself in a crevice among the rocks, was that snake, the cause of this crisis.

Claudius smoothed down his ruffled feath-ers and vowed not to lose his temper. You are a Bald Eagle, Claudius, he warned himself: maintain your dignity.

Two or three hops brought him within

speaking range.

'Well! You really did it this time, didn't you, Curly, you Snake-in-the-grass,' he said as pleasantly as possible.

Curly-Wurly raised her head and peered about cautiously. Her forked tongue flickered as if she expected trouble. Jimmy Racoon left off chatting to some squirrels in order to watch and listen. This was promising. There was a strong possibility of some excitement in the immediate future.

'I beg your pardon?' said Curly-Wurly.

'I said,' continued Claudius, 'that you really stirred it up good and proper, didn't you, you twister.'

'Stirred up ... what?'

'Stirred up the mud! Stirred up Trouble. I'm talking about Moose.'

'What about him?'

'I'll tell you what about him,' screeched Claudius. 'After five minutes' chat with you about his image he hates himself and wants new head-gear – *that's* what about him!'

Jimmy Racoon and the squirrels began to gather in a discreet circle. Nothing brightened their day like a real good row, and they knew when a war was coming.

'I'm afraid you've got completely the

wrong idea,' snapped Curly-Wurly. 'For your information Edward has been dissatisfied with his image ever since he saw those Yellow Monsters in the wood. Before that, even! Certainly long before he talked to me. Ask any of these folk and they'll tell you. He wants to be a more colourful personality.'

Claudius stretched out an accusing wing. It fairly trembled with rage.

'You told him to change his antlers. I know it was you. "Go see the Ugly Troll," said you. I'd like to wring your neck only I wouldn't know where to start. Because you're all neck, one big long neck and nothing else, that's you.'

'Jealousy will get you nowhere, Vulture,' said Curly-Wurly, sliding away.

'I AM A BALD EAGLE, NOT A VULTURE,' screeched Claudius, who was hopping on the spot. 'Come back here and say that to my face.'

Curly-Wurly, who was not a coward, turned, came back, and said 'Vulture,' to Claudius Bald Eagle's face: whereupon Claudius removed a beakful of flesh from her middle region.

'Mmm,' said Claudius, swallowing, 'a little dry, but not unpleasant.'

Curly-Wurly immediately straightened herself and sank her fangs into a feathery leg. And that was it. Within a blink of an eye they were at one another, beak and fang.

Jimmy Racoon and the squirrels could scarcely believe their luck. The beavers, similarly delighted by this turn of events, left off their construction work to sit on a log and cheer. None of them was particularly fussy who won the fight – they supported the one who happened to be on top.

At first Claudius took hold of the snake with one spiked foot and gave her a real good shake, only to be sent staggering by a bite in the shoulder. Then Curly-Wurly wrapped herself round the Bald Eagle and got ready to squeeze, only to receive a mighty blow above the eye from that wicked beak. The excitement proved too much for Jimmy Racoon, who swallowed his tongue and had to receive First Aid from Quincy Porcupine. He almost missed the finish of the fight. The hopping eagle and the writhing snake came together one last time, rolled across some open ground and bashed heavily into a rock together.

Now, in a flurry of dust, they came apart. Claudius, clearly dazed and dithery, flew up and away in ever-diminishing spirals to the

top of a distant tree, while Curly-Wurly rapidly slithered into a convenient crack in the ground.

The excitement was over. Each was bitterly ashamed not to have knocked the other creature senseless.

6

'Well Grace,' said Enid into the phone, 'I guess that's all the news. Oh, things are fine this end, just fine. The spiders are big but I just shut my eyes and step on 'em. The latest is, Harry wants to shoot a moose...

'Yes...

'Antlers, Grace, not horns...

'I don't know, like ordinary beef, I guess – I've never tasted moose. He's not going to eat it, you understand, he just wants the ... that's right, the antlers...

'Well I don't know which gun he'll use. His moose-gun, I suppose. You can get elephant-guns, can't you – why not moose-guns? Apparently this is a very large animal, Harry says he can't miss but you know Harry ... I hear him hammering outside, better go see what he's playing at. See you Monday, Grace – bye.'

Enid came off the phone after talking to her friend (long distance) for two and a half hours. With the TV and the phone, Enid felt very much at home. While Harry was heroically trying to get-away-from-it-all, Enid cheerfully brought-it-all-with-her.

The hammering outside grew louder and more insistent. She hurried through the spacious conservatory and out the back door to find that Harry was doing peculiar things to the car. The bonnet and radiator were now hidden under a huge network of bare branches, some of which had been sharpened to rather wicked-looking points. Also, a straw bale, marked with a colourful bull's-eye target, had been lashed between the headlights.

Harry greeted her with enthusiasm.

'Well? Don't you think it looks like a moose?'

'What?'

'The car, the car.'

Do I think the car looks like a moose, Enid repeated inwardly.

'No, Harry, I do not.'

'The branches are supposed to be antlers. Have you no imagination?'

With that retort, Harry picked up his gun,

strode purposefully down the drive, and lay down on the tarmac with the gun to his shoulder.

'Enid, get in the car. Start it moving in first gear and then jump out.'

'What are you going to do?'

'I'm going to shoot it.'

'The car?'

'Yes, the car, the car. But it'll be a *moose*, don't you see. And turn on the lights, they can be its eyes.'

Enid stood in front of the car with her bottom resting on the straw bale. She wanted more details about this crazy happening.

'You don't actually have real bullets in that thing, do you, Harry?'

'Of course I've got real bullets, how can I shoot something without real bullets, what?'

'But ... Harry, won't you destroy our lovely car?'

Harry jumped to his feet; he hated delays. 'I might have known you wouldn't understand,' he complained bitterly.

More calmly now, he tried to explain. 'Enid, I will not destroy the car. I will be shooting at the straw bale, how can I possibly destroy the car? The straw bale will *protect* the car.'

'But ... '

'Enid, my dear,' said Harry, 'I want you to picture me lying in that forest with a great brute of a moose charging straight for me. There is death in its eyes, Enid, it means business. This is not a picnic, this is for real. I mean, even blasted *actors* have rehearsals and they're only going on the blasted *stage!*'

It struck Enid most forcibly that there was no arguing with a man whose whole being was now infused with passion and unreason. Her protest, therefore, was a mild one.

'Harry,' she said, 'you are obsessed.'

'Just do it. And turn on its ey ... I mean *lights*.'

Enid did it, and turned on the lights. She jumped from the moving car and sprinted like a teenager into the safety of her home before Harry squeezed the trigger and let fly. I wish Grace were here, she thought – and the gun went off.

It was just horrendous. Enid saw the whole thing from the billiard-room window. The car-moose lost its antlers, blasted far and wide. The windscreen shattered into millions of little diamonds. The eyes – or, rather, the lights – first of all went out, then were blown off completely, and rattled down the drive as

if to escape from the bedlam behind them. And all the while the car-moose continued to chug towards Harry, who deftly rolled to one side and gave it a blast of both barrels up the rear.

It was safe to come out. Harry gripped Enid's arm in rapture. 'Enid, it's going to work! I know now that I can do it. Look!'

The stricken car-moose hit a tree in the distance, and gently turned right over with its wheels still spinning in the air.

Enid struggled to respond in some sensible way. She had just witnessed the Death of a Car-moose and the whole thing was larger than life, it was like something from the movies. She said, eventually, 'You're a millionaire, Harry, why don't you just buy antlers?'

'I got to shoot my own.'

'Get them second-hand, tell people you shot them yourself for heaven sakes, they'll never know.'

'You mean ... tell a *lie*?'

Enid sighed. 'Well Harry, if you ask me it beats being run over by a full-grown moose.'

7

Moose heard the whole story of the fight between Claudius and Curly-Wurly from Quincy Porcupine. Quincy told everything. She even described how she had saved Jimmy Racoon's life after he became excited and swallowed his tongue.

'You should not fight,' Edward told his friend. 'It never does any good. In fact it usually makes things much, much worse than they were and I am *very* surprised at you, Claudius.'

'I'm not speaking to you,' said Claudius from the third antler down.

'That's because you lost.'

'It was a *draw*!' shrieked Claudius. 'And listen who's talking. At least I don't frighten the life out of poor innocent alligators. *I* don't pick things up and throw them in the lake and try to drown them.'

Edward was momentarily embarrassed by this riposte.

'I wasn't feeling well that day, and I have apologised to Long Tom John for my behaviour.'

'I know,' said Claudius, 'I was there. He told you to get lost. And that's exactly what we are. Lost.'

They had arrived, after a morning's travelling, in the thickest shade at the deep heart of Thunder Wood. Although it was high noon and the sun shone brightly overhead, the sky seemed to twinkle like mere starlight beyond the dense canopy of leaves. And it was cool. Claudius shivered, but not entirely from the cold.

'Where does this Mr Gorgeous live anyway?' he asked, gloomily referring to the Repulsively Ugly Troll. 'This is a mistake, let me tell you. He'll have us for breakfast.'

'I don't think so,' said Edward.

'How do you know? Do you know what he eats? Raw meat, probably.'

'I must say, Claudius, it's very good of you to come with me,' Edward said sincerely. 'I do appreciate it.'

'I'm your pal, that's what pals are for,' replied Claudius, who was almost in tears when he imagined how generous and noble he must sound.

Actually, he still hoped to change Edward's mind at the last minute, he hadn't come on this trip just to be a nice guy. The oakleaf bandage round his left leg – where Curly-Wurly had bitten him – was intended to win sympathy. Claudius, who was a very fine actor, screwed up his face in agony when he thought Moose was watching.

And now, without warning, the sun came flooding through a gap in the trees with the precision of a great spotlight, and illuminated that particular clearing which was the dwelling-place of the Repulsively Ugly Troll. Claudius felt his heart throb. They had arrived.

They noticed, first, a silken sign which seemed to have been spun by legions of obedient spiders.

BALFOUR SCABIOUS, REPULSIVELY UGLY TROLL

Beyond, a line of washing fluttered outside a tumbledown shack with a single chimney at one end of the roof. A hammock had been slung between two great redwood trees, and this hammock was empty except for — curiously — a massive sledgehammer. The pall of bluish smoke which pervaded the whole scene came from a black cauldron, whose contents simmered quietly over an open fire.

Claudius took one sniff of this bubbling goo and almost passed out.

'Hnuff. HNUFF!' he said (trying to expel the smell from his nose). 'Oh boy. HNUFF! Okay, Moose, that's it, we've seen enough. Home time.'

'No,' came the answer.

'*Smell* that stuff. It is *vile*. I bet he uses it for spells.'

Edward took a sniff, and staggered backwards. Craftily, Claudius saw his chance.

'See? He'll make you drink that poison. Do you want to change your image that bad? No fear. Let's go home, pal, you can see he's not in.'

As if to prove him wrong, a grotesque knobbly hand suddenly trust itself out of the chimney of the shack – and that hand was holding by the neck a squawking hen.

Two more hens and a fine rooster with a beautiful red comb were evacuated from the shack through the same exit.

'AND STAY OUT OF MY FEET WHEN I'M SHAVING!' roared a terrible voice.

Balfour Scabious, Repulsively Ugly Troll, was very much at home.

8

'Yoo Hoo-oooo. Is anyone there?' called Edward. 'Mr Tro-ooll.'

'WAIT A MINUTE,' came the reply from inside the shack, 'I'M SHAVING RIGHT NOW.'

Claudius, who was already sitting back-to-back on Moose's antlers, gulped with fear. Never, never mess about with magic, he was thinking.

'Ed, old pal, let's go. This guy pushes chickens up chimneys, he scares me. You are a very fine moose, really.'

'Except for my antlers,' said Edward.

In any case it was too late to run. The door of the hut opened and a deep, cindery voice sang out this warning: 'I'm coming out now, folks, better cover your eyes. I'll walk out backwards of course, but even so, some folk find me shocking.'

57

Claudius stuck his head under a wing as the voice came closer.

'Sorry about the delay, folks, I had to finish my shave.'

'I d-d-didn't know that T-Trolls shu-shu-shaved,' stammered Claudius.

'I shave all over twice a day. If you think it's easy, try shaving behind your knees some-time.'

'I'm sure it's very difficult,' said Edward.

Claudius was dying to know what the Troll looked like. 'Just one peep,' something seemed to whisper in his ear, 'he's got his back to you, after all. And he can't be *that* ugly.' Squinting through a gap in his feathers, he saw a pair of ears like giant sea-shells, one of which boasted a large, round ear-ring. Then Claudius almost fell off his perch. Bal-four Scabious had an eye in the back of his head, and that blob of soft jelly was looking directly back at *him*.

'Look, let us get something straight,' said the Repulsively Ugly Troll with great patience, 'I am *not* a pretty sight. One look at me and you'll never be the same again so don't say you haven't been warned. Now what can I do for you folks?'

Carefully and with candour, Edward

explained how he had not been happy with himself for some time now; that he felt colourless, drab and boring and desperately in need of a change. It was quite a long speech.

'I have come here in search of self-improvement,' he finished eventually, 'and I think that I would like something different for my head.'

'You've got antlers,' said the Repulsively Ugly Troll, 'be happy with antlers, that's my advice.'

'Exactly what *I* said!' cried Claudius. His voice sounded muffled since it came from under his wing.

'I would like something a little more colourful,' persisted Edward, 'like ... like that rooster sitting on your roof, for example. Look how it has a wonderful red bit along the top of its head.'

Balfour Scabious raised a thorny brow and his third eye blinked in surprise.

'You want a red comb? Like a chicken?'

'Something nice and bright like that. Is it possible?'

'Anything's possible. Hold on there a minute and I'll get my book of spells.'

There now occurred a pause while the Troll leafed through the pages of a large book,

59

muttering, 'Nobody wants magic any more. Science, that's all they think about. A for Angel, B for Bow-wow, C for . . . Huh. I don't see anything here about chicken combs, that's mighty peculiar.'

'Try under H for Hen,' suggested Claudius.

'Mind your own business. Ah! Here we are. Spell 308. Okay, Moose, I can give you a comb without any bother, but it'll be ordinary hen-size, that's the problem.'

'That would be rather small,' agreed Edward.

It was obvious that an ordinary hen-sized comb would be rather tiny for Edward's large head. Suddenly a flash of inspiration lit up the black and orange eyes of the Repulsively Ugly Troll.

'Wait a minute! What am I thinking of! Sure I can always enlarge it when you've got it, enlarging things is easy. This is as good as done, folks – one Moose-comb coming up!'

First, though, Claudius had a question. 'Eh . . . excuse me,' he said timidly, 'can I ask you something?'

'Certainly.'

'Can you tell us whether this operation is reversible?'

'What do you mean, reversible?'

'I mean can he get his antlers back if he doesn't fancy looking like a chicken?'

Balfour Scabious seemed quite overcome by the idea.

'No no. No no no, oh no. This is a one-way ticket, Moose, there's only one thing that will bring your antlers back, and I've never known it to happen before.'

'What is it?' asked Claudius.

'Well, Moose, one of your close friends, somebody who genuinely thinks the world of you, has to come and look me in the face. And I am *not* a pretty sight. Unless you've got a friend like that, Moose, you can't get your antlers back.'

'I understand,' Moose said gravely, 'but I think that red will suit me very well.'

There now followed some fancy rhymes and runes from the Repulsively Ugly Troll. As spell 308 began to take effect, a gush of white mist developed around Moose and obscured his bulky shape so that he could scarcely be seen. The panicking Claudius took fright in case *he* should be included in the spell, and bolted to the top of the nearest tree in a straight line. When the vapours cleared away, it became obvious that the great span

61

of antlers had utterly gone; and instead, a long and floppy comb, exactly like a rooster's only much enlarged, ran down the middle of Edward Moose's skull.

Claudius unfolded his wings and risked a peep. 'Oh man,' he said to himself, not for the first time, 'this is serious!'

9

That same morning Harry got up so early he beat the sun out of bed.

His stomach, never demanding first thing in the morning, was well contented with the fruit juice, scrambled egg and coffee that the maid rustled up for him. He had just finished breakfast when Enid came into the kitchen wrapped up in her dressing-gown and wearing sloppy slippers on her feet.

'Oh! You should have stayed in bed, honey,' he said fondly, 'I didn't mean for you to get up.'

'I'll fix you some sandwiches.'

'One of the maids can do that.'

'It's your big day, Harry, the least I can do is fix you some sandwiches. I dare say you can get hungry waiting for a moose.'

Soon it was time. Harry dressed himself up in his hunting jacket, his cap, his knee-high boots, and threw a cartridge belt over one shoulder.

'Well?' he asked. 'What do you think?'

She thought that he looked like something out of the Magnificent Seven or Rip Van Winkle. 'I guess you'll do fine, Harry,' she said. They walked together to the end of the garden, and Harry disappeared into the forest with the gun broken over his shoulder.

On the way back to the house Enid passed the kidney-shaped, heated, outdoor swimming pool. Why, she wondered, did people build pools the shape of people's kidneys? It seemed like a silly thing to do. There were millions of shapes in the world, why pick kidneys? Enid decided to have a swim.

She was right in the middle of the pool when she heard the scuffling noise. Good glory, it's a bear at last, she thought. Then she saw it. Her heart stopped beating, she froze, there were creepy-crawlies in her scalp, she opened her mouth but no sound came out. As Enid watched Long Tom John the Alligator slide into her kidney-shaped swimming pool she felt like a movie actress giving a totally unconvincing performance.

Maybe, she thought, it's not real. Maybe it's a big rubber alligator, Harry's idea of a joke.

She was still screaming – and so were the maids – when they hauled her out of the water.

'I do not care what you say,' said Edward, 'so please stop talking. I don't think I'm boring to look at any more. Red suits me, and for the first time in my life I feel interesting.'

They were returning home along a path that ran parallel with the river close by. Claudius floated downstream on a very convenient log, keeping pace with Moose. (He still wore his oak-leaf bandage and claimed that he was far too lame to walk.) As Edward pranced along with his head held high, his new comb flopped first to one side and then to the other.

Claudius said, in a fit of pique, 'Right. You are quite right, you don't look boring, I admit it. Nobody would look at you and say, "There goes a boring Moose."' Claudius began to screech. 'YOU LOOK RIDICULOUS. You look like a big chicken. If you saw yourself you'd stick your stupid head in the nearest hollow tree!'

When it became obvious that such outbursts were getting him nowhere, Claudius brought the tip of his wings together to beg for mercy. 'Ed old buddy, please – let me ride on your back.'

'No,' said Edward firmly, 'your feet are too sharp.'

'My feet are too sharp,' repeated Claudius. 'My feet are too sharp. After all we've been through together and my feet are too sharp. My leg is in agony, my bandage is slipping and he says my feet are too sharp. Nobody loves you when you're down and out – boy is that a true saying!'

Claudius did not know it yet, but there was even worse to come. He was not, in fact, floating downstream on a log; he was floating downstream on the back of Long Tom John the Alligator – who, having failed to eat Enid early that morning, was still looking for his first meal of the day in the afternoon. Long Tom John sank out of sight ever-so-slowly, thereby allowing the cool and quickly-flowing water to lap round Claudius's lower regions.

'Hey!' Claudius said indignantly. 'How come my feathers are wet?'

He soon found out. Long Tom John was gone only for a moment, for a pair of jagged-toothed jaws suddenly broke through the sur-

face of the water with a terrifying roar, and Claudius was looking all the way down Long Tom John's red and purple throat.

Claudius always claimed, afterwards, that he was right inside that awful creature's mouth. Right in! Sheer terror caused him to walk on water in spite of his lame leg. Then he performed a vertical take-off as those jaws closed on his tail feathers with a blood-curdling snap.

Oh boy! moaned Claudius. He headed for the safety of the high and beautiful pines.

Claudius Bald Eagle had missed death by the skin of an alligator's teeth, and he now felt entitled to lose his head completely. 'See what you've done!' he cried out in rage at Long Tom John. 'My feathers, my lovely, lovely feathers, I hope they choke you, I hope they turn you into handbags and cowboy boots. I hope you're happy,' he bawled hysterically at his former friend Edward Moose. 'Now you can be happy, now you can smile, you almost got me eaten. BWAAAK!'

Edward Moose had seen nothing of all this – he had turned down a woodland path but a few moments before. Along this path, unknown to him, lay a man in a Davy Crockett hat with rifle at the ready.

The hide in the woods was really quite comfortable. It was made from bent saplings and woven leaves and carpeted with dry ferns as set out in Harry's personal copy of *Everything You Need To Know About Big Game*.

His rucksack contained a spy novel, corned-beef sandwiches and a dozen cans of beer – Harry knew that he might have to wait all day for that moose to come by.

69

Another man might have been lonely in such a wild place, but not Harry. He had company in a sense, for he talked to himself.

Should I smoke a cigar?

No.

Why not?

The moose'll smell it, Harry, that's why not.

About mid-afternoon, after his seventh can of beer, Harry heard the thrashing of a heavy body in the undergrowth. And it was coming closer!

The time was come. His heart suddenly began to shift blood all over his body in such quantities that even his trigger finger trembled. As the lumbering beast came closer, excerpts from Harry's childhood flashed before his eyes. What was life, he thought, what had it been but a long preparation for this short moment, him by himself alone against the majestic forest beast.

Stand firm, Harry.

My mouth has gone dry!

Forget your mouth, here it comes.

I hear it, I hear it.

Don't louse it up, now.

I won't, I won't.

Heart then head, Harry; heart then

head.

Now, Moose, *now*! I'm ready for you.

Harry had steeled himself to face a thing with eight foot antlers and death in its raging eyes. Instead, aiming through one eye, he saw a moose wearing a comb. A floppy red comb. It pranced through the open glade like a carefree giant chicken.

Harry blinked with both eyes, and looked again. His body gave a nervous little jerk. Unless he was very much mistaken, that Moose had a smile upon its face.

When it had gone – a matter of seconds, merely – Harry mopped his brow with a hanky and lit a cigar in the hope that this would steady his nerves. He abandoned his rucksack, his rifle, his novel and his beer; and then, talking away to himself, he headed roughly in the direction of home.

Man, that was real weird.

Did you see its headpiece, Harry? I kid you not, that was a chicken's comb.

No.

Yes. And it was smiling, Harry. *Smiling* ...

10

When Harry got home Enid was curled up in an armchair with the phone in one hand and a sweet Spanish sherry in the other.

This was not her first sherry. She'd put away quite a few since her swim that morning.

'Oh look,' she said brightly, 'it's Harry home at last. Hi, Harry, Grace sends you her love, she wants to know have you shot yourself a moose yet?'

'No,'

'No, Grace, he hasn't. He's mooseless. There's a mighty funny look in his eye, though, I guess he must have missed.'

'I did not miss.'

'He didn't miss, Grace. I suppose it's still lying out there. Harry ... ?'

'What?'

'Grace says something will eat it if you leave it out all night. And where is your moose-gun?'

Harry ran his fingers through his hair and left it standing on end. 'Enid, listen, I didn't shoot. The moose I saw ... ' Harry swallowed. 'The moose I saw had a ... a chicken's head.'

'A chicken's head?'

'A CHICKEN'S HEAD. And it was ... smiling.'

Enid stared up at Harry out of rather rounded eyes and quietly took a sip of sherry before resuming her chat with her friend. 'Grace, he says he saw a moose, but it had a chicken's head and it was smiling. Yes. Probably looked too cute to kill. Seems like he shot up the car for nothing. Hold on, I'll ask him.'

Enid tucked the phone under her chin. 'Harry, Grace says why don't you lay down your arms and take up golf?'

A distant and rather dreamy look had come into Harry's eyes, as if some kind of reaction were only now setting in.

'Enid honey, I think I'll go upstairs and lie myself down for a piece.'

'You go ahead, Harry,' Enid called after him. 'And by the way, I almost got eaten today. By an alligator.'

There was no reply from upstairs.

News travelled faster than a forest fire in Thunder Wood. The sad truth is that many spectators were already tittering out loud even before Edward Moose's first public appearance in his new headpiece.

Hundreds of squirrels chittered in the trees; beavers waited expectantly on their log; porcupines and weasels arrived breathlessly from other territories; migratory birds broke

flight to rest a while by the lakeside – all for a glimpse of the great-crested wonder.

'I don't believe a word of it, you know,' Curly-Wurly said to Quincy Porcupine and Jimmy Racoon. 'It's a rumour. Not even a moose could be so stupid.'

'Maybe not,' said Jimmy Racoon, 'but some squirrels have seen him and they're all saying it's true.'

'Squirrels!' Curly-Wurly sank contemptuously into coils. 'What do they know?'

'What about Long Tom John,' said Quincy. '*He* saw Moose and why would *he* tell a lie?'

'It's obvious. That alligator has been trying to get his own back since Edward threw him in the lake. No. It's absolutely out of the question.'

75

Then Edward stepped proudly into view, and they saw that it was true. There were incredible scenes. From the highest branch of the highest pine, Claudius Bald Eagle saw everything and heard it all. There were cries of 'Cock-a-doodle-dooo!' and 'Lay us an egg!' More than one helpless squirrel slipped head-long from the trees. Jimmy Racoon stretched himself out on the ground, for he was weak and wet-eyed, and had not laughed so dangerously since Long Tom John bit his own tail because he thought it was a fish. As for that alligator, *he* lay on the bank with his belly turned up to the sky and sounded out vulgar, throaty guffaws.

Motionless in the heights, Claudius Bald Eagle surveyed these happenings in the theatre below with glittering eyes. For just a moment he became his silly big friend Moose, and knew what Edward must be feeling. The Bald Eagle, for the first time in his life, experienced the pain of someone else.

Edward, meanwhile, was desolated. Their laughter struck him like unrelenting blows. 'Red Ed!' he heard them roar. 'Ed the Red!' Worse still, when Edward bent to drink and saw himself reflected in the surface of the water, he realised that he only had himself to blame for all this. There was a great empty space where his antlers had once spread over the water. He had not succeeded in improving himself at all, he merely looked ridiculous. As his big body heated up with shame, he wished only that he could melt away to nothing, and be all gone.

'You deserve this, Edward Moose,' he said to himself. Then he walked deep into the forest to be alone.

It was an hour later. Claudius Bald Eagle observed his large friend from a long way off. Moose stood forlornly under an ancient oak tree.

Claudius, at that moment, could not easily understand his feelings, he was all mixed-up. Normally he loved to gloat and say things like, 'I told you so, sucker,' but he didn't feel that way this evening, there was a lump in his throat. He swooped, and landed in a branch at Edward's head.

'Hi there, Moose, how's it going, then?'

Moose seemed surprised to see him. He stared blankly for a while, then said, 'All right, I suppose. How's your sore leg?'

'Oh ... ' Claudius was slightly embarrassed. His leg had never been sore. 'I took the bandage off. It's ... much improved.'

'I'm very glad. Were you down by the lake? Did you see what happened?'

Claudius tried to think of a joke. He failed, and just nodded.

'They called me Red Ed. They said ... they told me ... they shouted 'Lay us an egg'.'

'I know, pal, I know,' said Claudius gently, for his heart was breaking. The tear-drops rolling down his large friend's face were big enough to drown in.

'Anyway you were right,' said Edward, sniffing, 'about my antlers.'

'Forget it, pal,' Claudius advised grandly. 'Life is not always sunshine and sweet grass.'

'No. But I should have been content the way I was. You are my true friend, Claudius, and I should have listened to you – I see that now. Goodbye.'

Where are you going? Claudius almost asked him. But he knew there was no answer to the question. Moose simply wandered off aimlessly, his head following his feet.

11

Claudius Bald Eagle sat in the bole of a yew tree and said, 'Okay you guys, gather round and listen, this is serious.'

With these words, he began the meeting which he had hastily arranged among the friends of Edward Moose. Curly-Wurly was there with Jimmy Racoon, Beaver and Quincy Porcupine. Claudius lost no time in laying before them all the details of how Moose had lost his antlers, and how he must get them back again.

'There it is,' he finished. 'We've got to help Moose. One of you has to go face the Repulsively Ugly Troll and everything will be back to normal. Who's it gonna be?'

He eyed each of the potential volunteers in turn. They stared back as if he were crazy.

'One of us? One of *us*?' said Beaver. 'And what about *you*?'

'Well, you've been his friend longer than I have,' Claudius pointed out reasonably.

'Listen, Bird,' said Jimmy Racoon, who had a hot temper, 'I blame you. *You* made Moose miserable, there was nothing wrong with him until you arrived out of the sky. Huh. Carrying you about all day would make anybody miserable.'

'*I* certainly cannot go,' said Beaver. 'I'm on my lunchbreak and there's work to be done. There is always work to be done.' And she hurried away to chew up some trees.

'Count me out,' said Jimmy Racoon. 'If you want my opinion, Moose will soon get used to looking like a chicken. Be seeing you.'

Claudius had high hopes as he turned now to good old Quincy Porcupine, who was known to have some very fine qualities. 'What about you, Quincy? The Troll doesn't look so bad, I've seen him ... sort of.'

'I'm a mother,' said Quincy. 'Are you?' With these powerful words, she waddled away, leaving Claudius alone with his old rival, Curly-Wurly.

'What about you?' he said to the snake. 'Maybe you could talk to the Troll, make him understand that Moose just made a mistake.'

'No. No, I don't think so.'

'Why not?'

'I suppose that I could easily argue the pros and cons of the case, but...'

'But what? Are you a mother too?'

'No,' said Curly-Wurly philosophically, 'I'm just plain scared.'

Claudius, left perched on his own in the bole of the yew tree, sat very still with hooded, pensive eyes. After thinking deeply for some time, the Bald Eagle saw what he must do.

Balfour Scabious of Thunder Wood rolled out of his hammock in the morning and yawned a yawn which would have turned a hippopotamus green with envy. Unfortunately the yawn dislocated his jaw. *Click* it went, out of place.

What a bother, thought Balfour. Every morning in life the same thing happened. However, after a quick tap on the chin from the sledgehammer (kept there for exactly that purpose) he was right as rain and ready for the new day.

First he wakened the pets who slept in the hut. He stuck the hens up the chimney as usual (they liked to sit on the roof), chased the polecats out the window, shifted the family of porcupines from his easy chair and

81

tucked blankets round the two cuddly bear
cubs sleeping in his bed. (Balfour had found
them in the woods. He was now their foster-
father.)

Through the eye in the back of his head, Balfour observed the goat chewing the stuffing from the mattress, and realised that he felt hungry himself. So he put the cauldron of porridge on to boil and stirred it occasionally with his left foot.

After breakfast it was time for personal grooming. Balfour enjoyed a warm bath in a tin tub. He shaved all over, polished the knob on the end of his tail with the wire brush, and clipped his thorny eyebrows with heavy-duty secateurs. He was examining his wart-infested tongue in the mirror when a knock occurred at the front door.

A nervous bald eagle was standing there with its eyes shut.

'Do come in,' said Balfour Scabious.

Quite frankly, Claudius was quaking.

Every feather quivered as he perched on the goat's left horn. (This was sheer habit.) Claudius, Claudius, what are you doing here with this *beast*? he said to himself. Why are you risking a fate worse than death just to help a blasted moose? He no longer understood himself at all.

The Troll's voice made him jump. 'Are you sure you want to go through with this, Bald

Eagle?'

No I'm not, thought Claudius, panicking. He said, 'Tell me something, will you? What'll happen to me when I ... you know ... when I ... ?'

'Look into my face? Oh, it depends. You could turn into a column of stone, or a rather nice fossil, or a pillar of salt...'

Claudius groaned. A pillar of salt!

'... Mind you, I can't harm the really nice folk of this world, the honest and the true. But if your reasons are selfish reasons – if you want Moose to have his antlers back so that you can have free transport for the rest of your life, then you've had your chips, mate. Whoosh! Maybe Moose will get his antlers back, but it's bye-bye Bald Eagle. I am really very, *very* ugly.'

Claudius hopped from left to right, deftly changing horns. The window, he noticed, was wide open, he could fly away, now, back to safety. Find another Moose! Live long and be happy! Then there came into his head an image of a large, drab Edward wandering through the forest with that thing on his head, looking so ridiculous that he was laughed at by alligators. Blasted alligators!

'Look,' he said desperately, 'maybe I do

want a free ride, I don't know any more. But Moose is my friend and he's going to pieces and I have to straighten him out. So come on, Gorgeous, cut out the chat and turn round. I want to get this over with.'

'I'll say this for you, Bald Eagle – you've got a lot of nerve.'

Balfour Scabious, Repulsively Ugly Troll, turned round.

It was the weirdest sensation. Claudius felt as though a tiny explosion of light happened in his mind, and took him over. The light brightened into a frothy whiteness, and then became a powerful, smooth and silvery wave which simply swept him up and away, and dumped him . . .

Well, he wasn't sure where it dumped him, exactly – Claudius lay unable to move while time passed him by: it might have been ten seconds, ten minutes, a week or a fortnight, he couldn't tell. Vague shapes flitted before his eyes, which refused to focus. Something licked him all over – something spongelike, and wet, and salty.

Salt! I'm a pillar of salt, thought Claudius. 'BWAAAK. I'M A PILLAR OF SALT, I'M A PILLAR OF SALT!'

'You're not a pillar of salt,' said a familiar

voice, 'you're among friends. And do stop licking him, Moose, it doesn't help at all.'

Claudius sat up. He saw Curly-Wurly and Jimmy Racoon. And there, too, was Moose, with a fine pair of antlers sprouting from his head. Edward looked happy.

'Ed! Hey look, you got your branches back!'

'Thanks to you, Claudius,' Edward said gravely. 'We know what you did – all of us know. You went to see the Magic Troll of Thunder Wood. You went back alone and you faced him with great courage. You are a wonderful friend, Claudius, and you are a magnificent Bald Eagle. We salute you.'

Claudius stood, flapped the dust out of his wings, and skipped up to Edward's highest antler.

'You are a very good judge of character, Moose,' he said without modesty. 'Let's go, pal. *Mush*!'

They disappeared, galloping, into Thunder Wood.

12

Thunder Wood still stands where it has always stood since the last glaciers melted, as wild and beautiful as ever.

They almost ran a pipe-line through that forest a few years back, but the project didn't go well and they decided not to bother. Some people claim that the surveyors saw an unspeakably ugly beast among the trees one day, and that this had something to do with their decision. However, you can be sure that Balfour Scabious does not figure in any of the official reports. . . .

You should know that Harry sold his thirty-two guns and bought himself a set of gold-plated golf-clubs instead. Now he and Enid shoot bogeys together.

Claudius Bald Eagle still rides imperiously on the antlers of his friend Edward Moose through the leafy tunnels of Thunder Wood:

although from time to time he flies down to pick a fight with Curly-Wurly or Jimmy Racoon.

And Edward? Well, Moose is a lot more contented than he used to be. He feels that he understands a little more about the art of being happy, and frequently reminds himself that life, with its ups and downs, cannot always be sunshine and sweet grass.

You can see more Magnet Books
on the following pages:

PETER DICKINSON

A Box of Nothing

When James slipped through the fence into the Dump, it had been almost pure impulse. His idea was to find the box of nothing, hide it and then pick it up later.

But it wasn't there. Instead, James saw a mauve and yellow cliff. It was a long way up the slope, further than from home to school, more than a mile. Frightened, he swung back to scramble through the fence and get away.

But the fence had gone . . .

SAM McBRATNEY

Zesty

10p a week to insure all your rulers, pens, pencils, dinner tickets, break biscuits and sweets. It seemed like a good idea. 10p a week against loss, theft or criminal damage. It was a *brilliant* idea.

Mandy Taylor, Shorty, Gowso, Knuckles and Legweak all thought so. But Penny Brown had her own ideas about any scheme run by the dreadful Jimmy Zest. One – nobody would get anything back; Zesty was too clever. Two ... IT WOULD GO WRONG.

The second collection of stories about the irrepressible Jimmy Zest and his dauntless companions.

'Delightfully comic tales ... sympathetic and credible'
THE GUARDIAN

'Utterly believable'
THE SCOTSMAN

HARRY GILBERT

Sarah's Nest

"My name is Sarah. Some weeks ago I was an ordinary fourteen-year-old, with lots of problems. Now I am unique."

When Sarah's mother walked out, leaving her daughter and husband to fend for themselves, Sarah was shattered. But her new friends helped her and it was with them that she began to study the ants' nest.

Then came the accident. While Sarah's body lay in a coma, she herself was in the Nest, thinking and feeling as an ant. Could she save the Nest from the fearful danger that confronted it?

And could she save her own life?

MICHAEL MORPURGO

War Horse

It is 1914. In England, Albert is growing up on a Devon farm with a young horse he calls Joey. In Germany, Friedrich works in his butcher's shop. In France, Emilie and her brothers play in their orchard. But the clouds of war are on the horizon and great armies are gathering their strength. Soon they will all be drawn into the nightmare of battle.

This is the story of Joey and the people whose lives he touches, as they struggle for survival in the blasted wilderness of the Western Front.

Runner-up for the Whitbread Award

More Fiction from Magnet Books

While every effort is made to keep prices low, it is sometimes necessary to increase prices at short notice. Magnet books reserve the right to show new retail prices on covers which may differ from those previously advertised in the text or elsewhere.

The prices shown below were correct at the time of going to press.

All these books are available at your bookshop or newsagent, or can be ordered direct from the publisher. Just tick the titles you want and fill in the form below.

MAGNET BOOKS   Cash Sales Department
                P.O. Box 11, Falmouth,
                Cornwall TR10 9EN

Please send cheque or postal order, no currency, for purchaser price quoted and allow the following for postage and packing;

UK   60p for the first book, 25p for the second book and 15p for each additional book ordered to a maximum charge of £1.90.

BFPO and Eire   60p for the first book, 25p for the second book and 15p for each next seven books, thereafter 9p per book.

Overseas   £1.25 for the first book, 75p for the second book and 28p for
Customers   each subsequent title ordered.

NAME (Block letters) ....

ADDRESS ....

....